HILARY & THE LIONS

Story by FRANK DESAIX

Pictures by DEBORAH DURLAND DESAIX

A SUNBURST BOOK ▸ FARRAR STRAUS GIROUX

To Pete and Chris and Preston and Kitty

On her first visit to New York City, Hilary held her parents' hands tightly. Skyscrapers shaded the streets they walked on. People and cars rushed everywhere. When a taxi honked too near, all three of them jumped, then giggled together.

Hilary freed her hands and stopped for a moment. Bright banners waved from buildings that rose like canyon walls till they squeezed the sky. The buildings' tops were so far up that they even seemed to sway a bit.

Hilary quickly looked back down, right into a masked face grinning at her. A giant panda sat in a toy-store window. Beside it, a shiny blue whale stood poised on its tail. She laughed and turned to her parents. But they weren't there.

Just legs.

Everywhere.

Hilary darted to the curb. Across the street was a huge library with long rows of steps, and two stone lions who looked out over everybody. She could see, and be seen, more easily from there.

When the rush of traffic paused, dozens of people crossed Fifth Avenue. Hilary joined them. She ran up the library steps and turned beside one of the lions. She still wasn't high enough to see over the crowd. But the lion on his pedestal was.

His tail lay just over the edge, a good handle to pull herself up with. So she did. She tried to look at every face that went by, and sighed. Perhaps her parents would spot her up there with the lion. While she waited, she brushed soot off his nose. Then she curled up and wondered what to do next. It was growing dark. At least she felt safe nestled between the huge paws. She imagined the lion even purred a little.

The purring would have been comforting if it weren't so loud. She opened her eyes to a cool night. The streets were empty and still. "Shhhh," rumbled the purr. "It's all right. It's just me." The mane softened and snuggled around her.

By now, Hilary was wide awake. "You're alive?"

"Getting there." The lion flexed his shoulders. His voice rumbled from his chest, grandfatherly. "Getting there very nicely, thank you." Hilary liked this creature. He sat up, and she dared to turn around. "I am Ainsley," said the lion. "My friend over there is Rollo."

Rollo had turned golden, too, and was stretching and yawning like a waking housecat. He carefully inched down his pedestal and finally leaped the last few inches to the ground. He walked toward them slowly, as if leading a parade.

"Can't other people see you?" Hilary asked Ainsley.

"If they wish to."

"Humans see what they wish to see," Rollo added as he reached them. "Imagination helps."

"You seem real to me," Hilary said. "You even smell the way lions should."

Ainsley chuckled. "Oh, we're real enough. If you'll climb up on my back, we'll join Rollo down there." As soon as she did, Ainsley leaped and landed softly. Rollo turned and sniffed her hair. "Don't worry. We'll get you unlost."

Hilary settled into Ainsley's thick fur. The two lions trotted, side by side, up the street.

Soon there were tree shadows and rolling meadows. The lions slowed, Ainsley knelt, and Hilary climbed off. "Central Park." Ainsley yawned. "A good place to rest in."

"And doze and dream in," said Rollo, as his friend flopped onto his back with a little grunt.

"I remember how we used to laze about at the old zoo," Rollo said, "and watch the children wish they were lions. Then the sculptor came and captured our spirits in marble and gave us the library to protect. Each year, we roam free, the length of Manhattan, this one magic night. We visit friends and sometimes make new ones." He looked at her and blinked slowly.

Ainsley rolled over. "Good memories make such good dreams," he said to Hilary. "But let's move on. Rollo's younger. You can ride him this time."

And what a ride it was. Rollo purred as if he had an engine in him. Hilary clutched his mane as the two great lions bounded past tree shadows back to the streets of New York. The lions trotted, and loped, and galloped. Once they leaped past an entire block in two strides. They raced down avenues and streets, past squares and greens, through places named Chelsea, Gramercy, Greenwich, and SoHo. Hilary's hair swirled in the rushing breeze. Then they stopped.

Hilary leaned over Rollo's head. A squirrel sat smack in front of them, nibbling a nut in its paws.

"Hello, Patrick." Rollo lowered his head. "Meet Hilary." Patrick stopped eating and looked up at Hilary. His eyes twinkled. He flicked his tail.

"Do you live here?" Hilary asked. Around them were only buildings of brick and stone.

"Yes, and my parents too, and their parents, too."

"But there are no trees."

"Oh, rainpipes and railings do fine. And ledges and eaves, and windowsills. Old buildings make fine trees."

Patrick scampered away, under a parked car, over a railing, up a downpipe, across a brick face, and along the roof line.

"Where's he going?"

Ainsley nodded toward the end of the street, where high in the air a long string of lights dipped and rose. The buildings on the way were hushed, sleeping. The lions padded softly toward the lights, Hilary still riding Rollo.

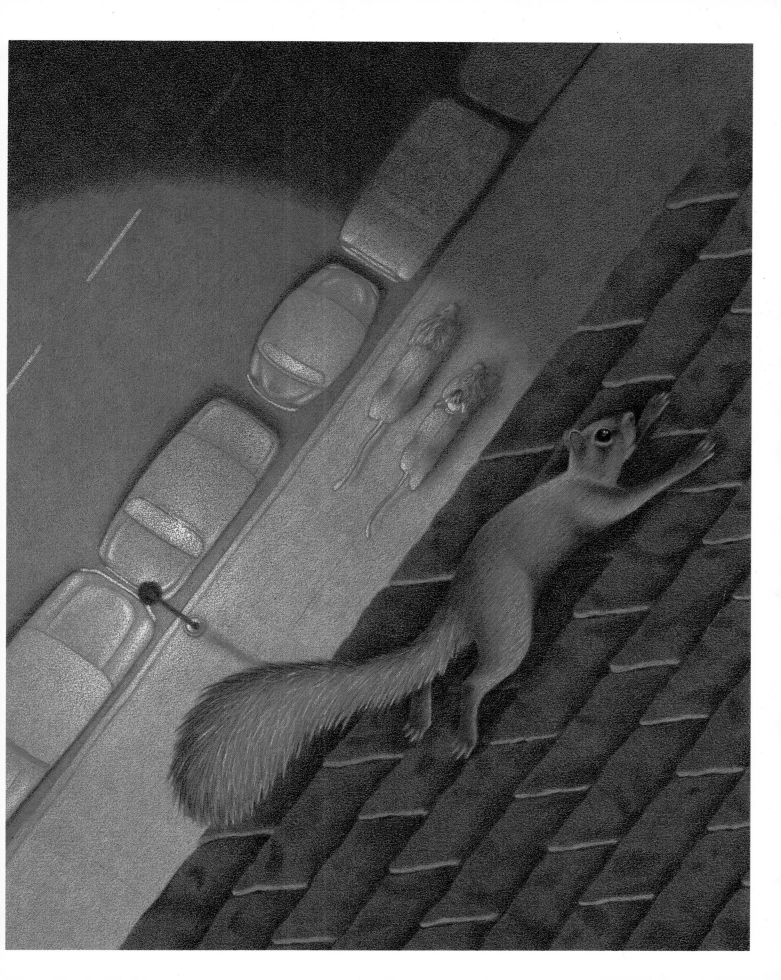

The lights, like two wonderful strings of pearls, rose to a point high in the sky, dipped down, rose again, then dropped away to the other side of the river. The Brooklyn Bridge hung under the lights. Hilary and the lions stood below it.

"Listen," whispered Ainsley. There were no cars, and no wind.

The bridge hummed.

Hilary cocked her head. The hum was like a beehive, far away.

"Is it alive?"

"Maybe." Rollo blinked, cat-like. "Maybe it's like us."

"Like everything," whispered Hilary.

Patrick sat on the rail, an ordinary squirrel, and flicked his tail twice.

Ainsley brushed Hilary with his whiskers. "Now it's time to go."

Hilary, Ainsley, and Rollo paused on the street outside Hilary's hotel. Through the window, Hilary saw her parents talking to policemen. She turned back to the lions and brushed Rollo's mane with her fingers. "What'll I tell them?"

"Tell them the truth," Ainsley purred.

And if a lion can smile, Rollo smiled.

Hilary told her parents the truth. Two friends, Ainsley and Rollo, found her and led her home — to them.

In a taxi to the airport the next morning, they passed the great bridge, buzzing with cars now. The city was alive with people again.

Their yellow taxi passed the library. Two stone lions guarded the steps leading to it. The lions glittered golden as they slowly passed by. Only Hilary knew it wasn't just the morning sun.